MY MOM IS SO FLY

JEROME STANISLAUS

MY MOM IS SO FLY

Copyright © 2020 by Jerome Stanislaus

DEDICATION

This book is to my daughters Jerney and Jesslyn. The world is yours! I love you.

"Are you working tonight, Mommy?"

"Yes, Pumpkin," Mommy said.

"I have an overnight flight. Daddy will take you to school in the morning, but I will be back in time to pick you up."

"Sounds like a plan!" I said.

"Daddy and I sing karaoke on the way to school."

Mommy smiled and said, "That sounds like fun!"

"Mommy, I have a question."

"I have an answer, Pumpkin."

"Did you always want to be a pilot?"

"Yes, for as long as I can remember."

"Did you ever dream of being anything else, like a nurse, a lawyer, or maybe a princess?"

"No, Pumpkin. My head has always been in the clouds."

"Mommy, is it easy to fly those big airplanes?"

"It wasn't at first, but I practiced, practiced, practiced."

Excitedly I asked, "Mommy, can you tell me the story of how you became a pilot, again?"

"I've told you this story so many times."

"I know, but I really want to hear it again."

"I want to hear it too!" said Dad.

"Okay, okay. Lucky for you two, I'm early."

Daddy and I cheered, "Yay!"

"It all started when I was about three years old. Auntie Jerney, Auntie Jesslyn, Grandma, Grandpa, and me went on vacation. It was my first time on a plane."

"Were you excited?" I asked.

"I don't remember," Mommy said. "But, according to Grandpa, he'd never seen me so excited."

"Mommy, what was your favorite part of the flight?"

"My favorite part of the flight was the takeoff."

"But now your favorite part is the landing, right?"

"Pumpkin, you know me so well," Mommy exclaimed.

Mommy continued telling her story.

"As I got older, my passion for the sky only grew stronger. Every time we drove past the airport, or I saw an airplane in the sky I got really excited."

"I would even watch birds in the sky, paying close attention to how they flapped their wings and moved their tails."

"After I did my homework, I would make paper airplanes and pretend to fly them to different airports around the world."

"One time, for Halloween, I even dressed up as a blind zombie-pilot. GRRR!" Mommy said in her best zombie voice.

"Ha! Ha! You were the scariest pilot in the sky," I said. Mommy laughed and said, "Yes, the scariest!"

Mommy continued.

"When I was 12, Grandpa bought me a flight simulator for my birthday."

"What is a flight simulator again?" I asked.

Mommy explained, "It's like a video game, but made to imitate real life."

"Was it like the real thing?"

"As close as I could get."

"Is that where you learned to land a plane so well?"

Mommy laughed and said, "Ehhh, I guess you could say that."

"Ok, finish telling me how you became a pilot, Mommy!"

"Alright, alright," Mommy said. "We had a career day in high school and a young woman who graduated just a few years earlier came in to talk about her job in the Air Force as a fighter jet pilot."

"She said that after she graduated high school, she went to college, then joined the Air Force to learn to fly. I was so inspired by her story that I wanted to be just like her. Especially since her hair was curly just like mine," Mommy chuckled.

"The only difference between her and I was that I wanted to fly families on vacations to tropical islands. So, instead of the Air Force, I signed up for flight lessons at a local flight school. That is where I earned all of my flying certificates. After that, I taught young men and women how to fly until I had enough flight hours to apply for a job at an airline."

"How many flight hours did you need?" I asked.

"I needed 1,500 hours," Mommy said.

I gasped. "Wow, that's a lot of hours. Was it expensive?"

"It was very expensive," Mommy said. "But I worked hard and my family all pitched in to help me."

"Mommy, were you ever scared?" I asked.

"Scared of what?" Mommy said.

"Scared that maybe you couldn't achieve your goal?"

"Hmmm, sometimes. But, Grandma and Grandpa always told me that I was not made of fear and that I had a strong mind. They told me that I could use my mind to control my fear. So, that is what I did. What made you ask me if I was scared?"

"I asked because my teacher said, "If your dreams do not scare you, they are not big enough." So, I wanted to see how big your dreams were."

"Well, in that case my dreams were terrifying!" Mommy said.

"Okay, Pumpkin," Dad said. "It's time for Mommy to go to work and time for you to go to bed."

I yawned. "Okay, Daddy. Goodnight and have a safe flight, Mommy!"

They smiled and said, "Goodnight, Pumpkin!"

Made in the USA
Middletown, DE
05 May 2022

65343833R00020